PAUL MORTON

BUG BELLY
BABYSITTING
TROUBLE

FIVE QUILLS

TOP POND

MIDDLE POND

OLD OAK

BUG BELLY
BABYSITTING TROUBLE

FIVE QUILLS

For my wife Janet, a constant support
and encouragement, and for Koray,
the original inspiration
for Bug Belly.

BUG BELLY: BABYSITTING TROUBLE
First published in Great Britain in 2020 by Five Quills
93 Oakwood Court, London W14 8JZ

www.fivequills.co.uk

Five Quills and associated logos are a trademark of Five Quills Ltd.

Text and illustrations copyright © Paul Morton

The right of Paul Morton to be identified as the author
and illustrator of this work has been asserted.

Edited by Natascha Biebow at Blue Elephant Storyshaping
Designed by Amy Cooper

A CIP record for this title is available from the British Library

ISBN 978 1 912923 04 5

1 3 5 7 9 10 8 6 4 2

Printed in Croatia by INK69

Can you find the HIDDEN worm in this book?

NEWT
ISLAND

WARNING

BOTTOM
POND

RIVER

BOGGY BOTTOM

BUG BELLY AND FROGLETS

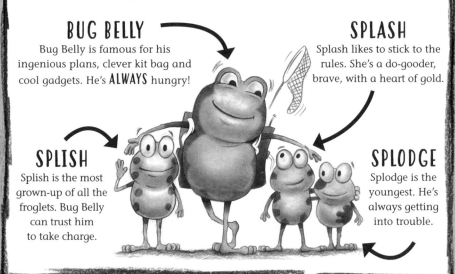

BUG BELLY

Bug Belly is famous for his ingenious plans, clever kit bag and cool gadgets. He's **ALWAYS** hungry!

SPLASH

Splash likes to stick to the rules. She's a do-gooder, brave, with a heart of gold.

SPLISH

Splish is the most grown-up of all the froglets. Bug Belly can trust him to take charge.

SPLODGE

Splodge is the youngest. He's always getting into trouble.

OLD SNAPPER

NAME: Pikus Horribilis

EATS: Anything slower

LIVES: Middle pond

FRIENDS: None

ENEMIES: None, not even fishermen

HERON

NAME: Froggius spearus
EATS: Taddies, froglets & fish
LIVES: No one is sure
FRIENDS: Some other birds
ENEMIES: Large foxes

SNEAKY SNAKE

NAME: Slytherus Sneakus
EATS: Tadpoles & froglets
LIVES: Sneaks around all 3 ponds
FRIENDS: Other snakes
ENEMIES: Owls and hawks

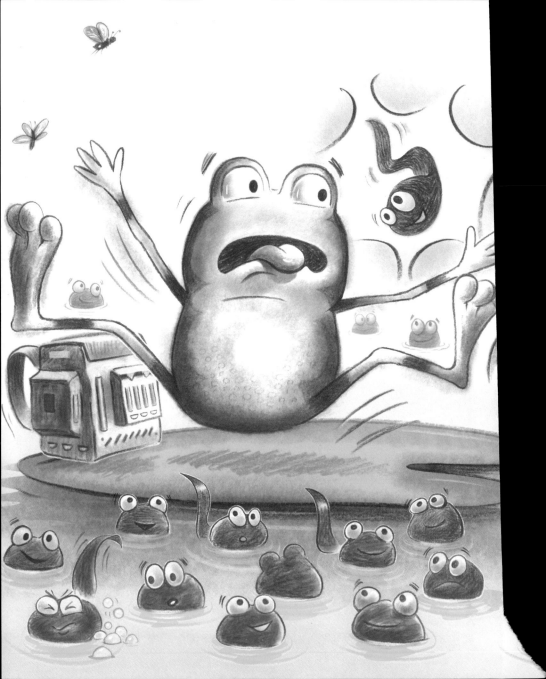

Chapter 1

SPLAAAATT!

Bug Belly was slapped awake by a slippery **SLOP** to the side of his face. It felt like being hit by a ginormous jelly. Before he had time to wonder who was flinging giant puddings about, there came a second **SPLOT!**

And then a third **SPLAAATT!**

A wet, sticky black blob bounced off Bug Belly's bonce. He sat up and looked around.

Then he looked again in amazement.

Bug Belly was surrounded by hundreds and hundreds of shiny black blobs. They were jiggling and giggling like a sea of black jelly beans coming to the boil.

"Come on, Uncle Bug Belly, **WAKE UP**, **WAKE UP!** We want to play," the tadpoles and little froglets shouted.

"Ah! Now I remember. Today it's MY turn to babysit." Bug Belly grinned. "Right you lot, gather round. First, let's make sure everyone is here."

He started to call out names. There were a LOT of names!

Olivia, are you here? Oh good. Leela? Yes! Zara, Rosie, Amber, Anya, Ayala. Come on, where are all the boys? Ben AND Benji? Both here. Sian, Dexter, Fadila, Caden, Sue. Sue! Pay attention please.

Darcie, Lou, Emile, Simone, Piper and Perry. Good. Jessica, Evie, Ava, Erik, Ivy, Harper and Phoebe, or is it Phoebe and Harper? Sorry, I always get you two mixed up. Flo, Matty, Amar, Vi, Amber, whoops already counted you. Tempest, Leaper, Abel, Chas, Corrie, Ifa and Afif, Lulu, Noah, Paula, Abu, Brad, Aisha, Scarlett, Penny, Zoe, Agnes, Grace, Gian, Nina, Jerry, Cherry, Kerry, Terry, Berry and Merry - oh, I see what you lot are doing.

Marlon, Plip, Frizzy, Plop, Jasmine, Kiki, Kris, Kanga, Izzy, Charlotte. Oh sorry you prefer Lottie now. Yes, I remember. Isla, Freya, Koray, Atlas, Bella, Rosie - what, again!? Hey, Rosie, don't keep moving around!

Hey, that's us!

Frans, Belinda, Will, Jaco, Leila, Pebble, Blue, Fannie, Leo, Emerald, Aria, Emma, Luna, Harry, Ron, Hermione, Hopper and Orla. Tambo, Aziz, Daphne, Fernando, Gwyneth, Janet, Diane, Sheena, Allegra, Chula, Serra, Violette, Natascha, Twyla, Sky, Morna, Lucas, Martin, Madison, Jazz, Juba, Asher, Isabella, Amara, Wyatt, Jack, Sophia, Baker, Milo, Lily and Lee.

Can you guess how many tadpoles and froglets there are? (Find the answer later in the story!)

Avery, Kyrie, Marley, Hayden, Joyce, Angel, Mina, Reese, Riley, Rory and River. Tad, Paul. Do you two always stand together? Rowan, Sam, Sawyer, Straw, Tatum, Kami, Devon, Tobin, Cho, Jordan, Zephyr - ooh what a nice name!

I'm Zephyr!

Efan, Abbie, Andie, Fran, Ruby, Mia, Chloe, Thomas, Cherie, Billi, Brandon, Vivian, Si, Poppy, Archie, Eddie, Splish, Splash and Splodge. I'm pleased to see you three - phew!

Indigo, Rio, Cleo, Ziggy, Sage, Taylor, Morton, Ariel, Parker, Finley, Dean, Katja, Ellis, Emery. Crikey, are we nearly done?

Quinn, Oakley, Grass, Reed, Eagle, Ezri, Atticus, Axel, Tommy, Craig, Guthrie, Glen, Harley, Jett, Morgan, Casper, Kes, Carrie, Moe, Nat, Fara, Hal, Abelia, Vernon, Cloud - stop wandering around by yourself, please! Daffodil, Daisy and Dahlia. Ah, yes, the triplets. Good.

Bobbie, Dazzler, Yana, Star, Ishaan, Fern, Bloom, Gina, Dina, Javan, Annisaa, Soma, Will, Barnaby, Muddle, Ping, Kamila, Rush, Puddle, Wiggle, Day, Night, Dylan, Lucy, Lola, Martha, Flip, Dori, Lennon, Pepper, Filipe, Aarav, Roly, Poly, Pudden and Pi.

"**Phew!**" Bug Belly let out a sigh of relief. "OK, listen up," he shouted, his mouth full of caterpillar chews. "The mums and dads have gone off to a frogspawn conference and I'm looking after you for the whole day."

"SO, WHO ... WANTS ... TO HAVE ... SOME ... FROGGY FUN!!!!"

"We do!" they all cheered excitedly.

Chapter 2

Bug Belly knew exactly what little taddies liked. With help from the older froglets, it wasn't long before he'd organised some fantastic water sports.

Of course there were slides.

WHEEEEE!

Some taddies played
water ball.

Others raced.

Bug Belly's tummy went

URGLE-GURGLE GLUMP!

It was the teeniest tummy grumble, but it spelled only one thing – TROUBLE!

You see, Bug Belly had one big weakness. He was **always** hungry! So, even though he was half-way down the water slide, he immediately started thinking about **lunch**.

He was already wearing his Sluggo Grip Mitt (always ready – just in case) and when he spied a particularly juicy slug below, launched himself off the slide, did a double somersault and . . .

. . . rocketed through the air straight towards it. In Bug Belly's head it looked something like this:

But it didn't turn out quite how
he'd planned . . .

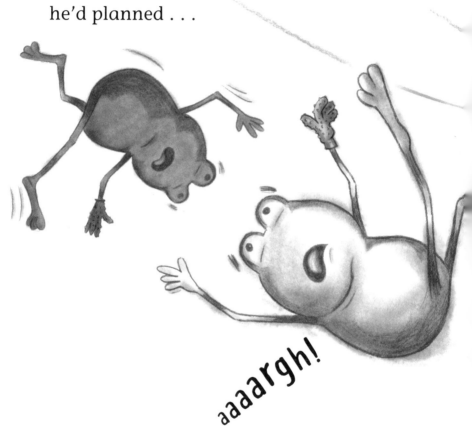

Although Bug Belly **DID** catch the slug, he crash-landed face-first into a fence post.

He hit it so hard that it knocked loose several rocks.

So now, where the rocks had been, there was a **BIG GAP**.

This might not seem like a big deal, but those rocks had been safely holding water in Top Pond for years. And now, they weren't.

Water gushed through the gap.

Top Pond was

EMPTYING!

Chapter 3

Bug Belly gulped. The little tadpoles hadn't yet grown their legs so they couldn't hop or jump. So, without any water to swim in they would be stranded and stuck helpless in the empty pond.

Bug Belly closed his eyes, and tried desperately to hatch one of his famous ingenious plans.

"Everyone, over here, please!" he shouted urgently to the young froglets and taddies.

"Oooh, have you thought of even more exciting rides?" they asked.

"No, yes, well, maybe, listen up, we have a problem. A BIG problem. Our pond is emptying! The water is draining away."

Everyone went quiet, except for three little frogs, Splish, Splash and Splodge.

Splish put up his hand. "Er, how?"

Then Splash piped up, "Yes, exactly **WHY** is the water running out?"

"Never mind about how and why right now," said Bug Belly. "Take it from me this is **SERIOUS**. We need to get everyone out of Top Pond and down to Bottom Pond as quickly as possible."

"But what about Middle Pond?" questioned Splodge.

"Yes, surely Middle Pond is much nearer," chipped in Splash.

Bug Belly sighed. He could tell this was going to be tricky.

"Well, you see, in Middle Pond . . . " continued Bug Belly, lowering his voice to a serious whisper so that even Splish and his friends suddenly went quiet, "there lives the most evil angry fish you'll ever meet – **Old Snapper.**

"He is one mean and hungry pike. He would gobble up you young frogs for starters, swallow **ME** whole for mains and top it all off with tadpole pudding!"

Splish gasped.

"What can we do, Uncle Bug Belly?"

OLD SNAPPER'S MENU

First course

Fresh young froglets served on a bed of green snotweed.

Main course

One juicy fat croaker served on a lily leaf.

Desserts

Tadpole Tapioca

"Middle Pond is far too wide to get around," said Bug Belly. "We can't go through it, so we'll just have to go **OVER IT!**"

"But how?!" asked Splodge.

"And what about Old Snapper?!" said Splish.

"We'll all be fish food!" cried Splash.

Bug Belly wracked his brain. How on earth could he achieve this impossible task? He munched on a water beetle snack to help him think. He was just about to get a really clever idea when a young frog came splashing frantically towards them.

Chapter 4

"Whaaat? Oh spitting speckled spiders," wailed Bug Belly. "Not Heron. Not today. Not now!"

The heron was the frogs' worst enemy. If you were caught by Heron you were a gonner. Plus very few saw her coming before they were going!

"Uncle Bug Belly, do something!" the tadpoles wailed.

What did he say?

Doesn't sound good . . .

Who's Helen?

I think he said 'Helen's a squirt!'

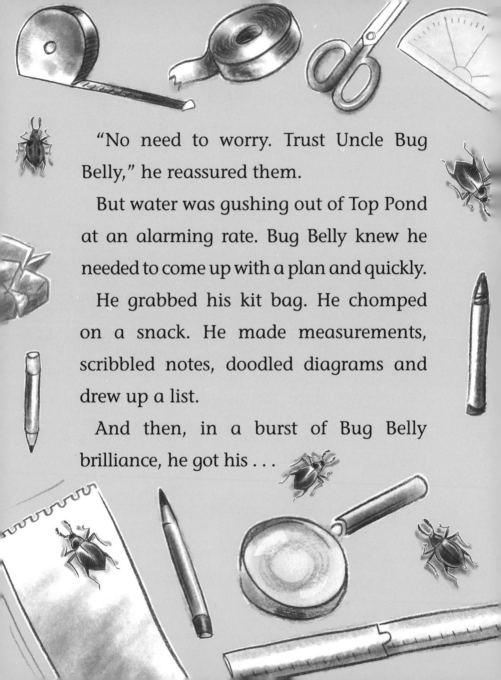

"No need to worry. Trust Uncle Bug Belly," he reassured them.

But water was gushing out of Top Pond at an alarming rate. Bug Belly knew he needed to come up with a plan and quickly.

He grabbed his kit bag. He chomped on a snack. He made measurements, scribbled notes, doodled diagrams and drew up a list.

And then, in a burst of Bug Belly brilliance, he got his . . .

very best ever clever idea!

So clever, in fact, that it needs to be split into three parts just to fit it into this story.

"OK, listen up," he said. "It's going to be tricky, it's going to be tight, but **THIS** is what we'll do."

Chapter 5

"**I**'ll take care of the **BIG** problems. What I need **YOU** all to do is quickly, and **VERY QUIETLY**, follow these instructions."

He handed Splish a list. It looked like the plans for the most fantastic water slide ever.

"Get busy building. There's no time to lose," said Bug Belly. "I'll be back as quickly as I can!"

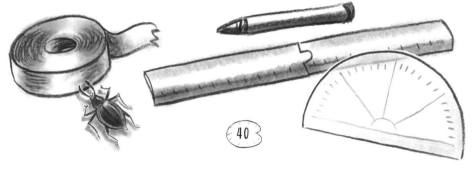

BUG BELLY'S CLEVEREST PLAN part 1

...cut   ...cut

Cut lots of hollow stalks.

edge of Top Pond = 2
over Middle Pond = 4

+   ✓

Need 6
in total   ⑥ ✓

into each other

Top Pond

to Middle Pond

DANGER
IMPORTANT

Hide
here!

If Heron finds you GO TO LOG!

"But . . . You can't leave us alone, not with Heron about," complained Splash.

"If Heron does find you, I've left instructions," said Bug Belly.

"But where are YOU going?" cried the taddies.

"Well, first, I'm off to pay Old Snapper a visit!"

There was a long silence as they all
pictured their uncle as Old Snapper's
lunch . . .

Chapter 6

Bug Belly was really worried. He knew that just like the water in Top Pond, time was running out. As quickly as he could, he emptied his kit bag and prepared the special items he needed for his **Cleverest Plan part 2.**

As usual, when he was working on a cunning plan, he spoke out loud to himself:

"First, collect and cut some hollow stalks. Now, slot these stalks together to make a long tube.

"Hmmm, let's see . . . where's my string? Tie it to this small stone and catapult it up and over that branch. Good. Next, peg the string tightly across Middle Pond.

"Ooh, yum, look, a tasty **bite-sized beetle** . . ."

Bug Belly stopped himself.

"No, No! No time for **snacks**!

"Finally, I need . . . ah, here's the perfect stick."

Now Bug Belly was ready. He didn't like heights, but he was determined. He shimmied up the string and headed out over Middle pond – Old Snapper's pond!

BUG BELLY'S CLEVEREST PLAN part 2

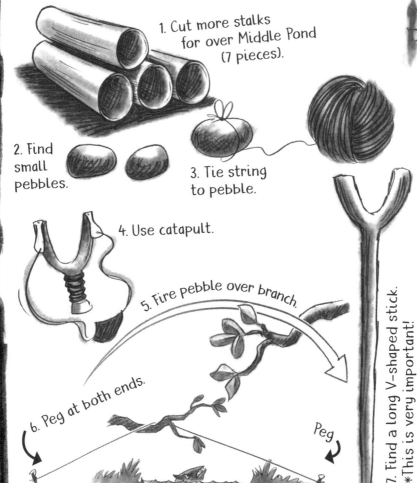

1. Cut more stalks for over Middle Pond (7 pieces).

2. Find small pebbles.

3. Tie string to pebble.

4. Use catapult.

5. Fire pebble over branch.

6. Peg at both ends.

7. Find a long V-shaped stick. *This is very important!

Peg

MIDDLE POND

Old Snapper had been cruising the edges of his pond all morning hoping to nab a napping newt or two.

He never saw Bug Belly arrive, but he heard a RUSTLING and then, an unusual twanging noise and some puffing.

Curiosity made him circle round.

He looked up and couldn't believe what he was looking at.

There, dangling in mid-air, was a fat, juicy frog. And not just any old frog! Old Snapper recognised that belly immediately.

"Well, lucky old me," he laughed. "Lunch on a line."

Smacking his lips he torpedoed towards the swinging frog.

But no matter how much Old Snapper arched and stretched out of the water he couldn't quite snap those tasty toes.

Bug Belly swung himself to the centre of the pond and lifted up the stick. Thinking he was about to be whacked, Old Snapper scarpered.

SNAP!

Laughing, Bug Belly slammed his stick down sharply into the water, like a spear. "Perfect," he said, zipping back across the pond.

He quickly hoisted the tube slide he'd made earlier on top of the stick. It now went all the way from Bottom Pond, over Middle Pond towards Top Pond.

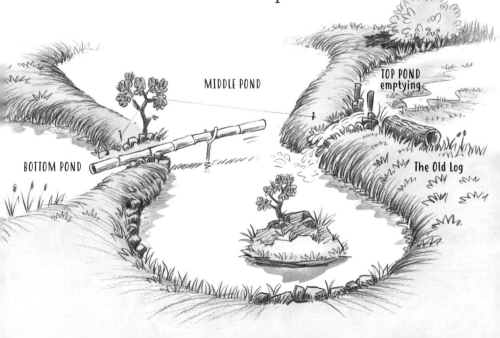

MIDDLE POND

TOP POND
emptying

BOTTOM POND

The Old Log

"That looks excellent! Now quick as a greased grasshopper back to the taddies." Bug Belly was just about to hop off when he heard

URGLE-GURGLE GLUMP!

Uh-oh . . .

Bug Belly thought about LUNCH.

Bug Belly thought about the taddies.

Bug Belly thought about the water draining away, and he raced back to Top Pond faster than he could slurp up a fly.

WHOOOOOSH!

A shadow swooped right over Bug Belly's head. He looked up and saw something that made his legs wobble. A large bird was heading straight for Top Pond.

"Aw Pickled Pond Skaters! **No, no, NO,** please, don't let me be too late!" he cried.

He couldn't see the taddies or froglets anywhere ... "Right come on, Bug Belly. There's no time to lose," he told himself.

"Think **QUICKLY**. How on earth am I going to scare that heron away?"

Chapter 7

Whilst Bug Belly had been cleverly outsmarting Old Snapper, the taddies and froglets had been carefully following their uncle's plans for the giant slide to Middle Pond.

"Here, help me," said Splish. "We're nearly finished."

They huffed and puffed and pushed the long tube out over the edge of Top Pond. Then they collapsed in a tired heap and waited anxiously for Bug Belly to return.

"W-w-what if Old Snapper m-m-munched him up in one b-b-big bite?" whimpered one taddie.

"Don't worry, Uncle Bug Belly's plans never ever fail," smiled Splish, reassuringly.

But just at that very moment there was a loud flip-flapping of wings!

"Oh, nooooo!" yelped Splodge. "It's Heron!! **HERON HAS COME!**"

Acting on Bug Belly's instructions, Splish took charge.

"Over to that log! Go, go, GO!" he shouted.

Quick as they could, the taddies waggled and wiggled their way to the safety of an old hollow log.

It wasn't easy now that the pond was more mud than water.

The tadpoles tried their best to be quiet, but their hearts were thumping. Then they saw Splodge, still squelching through the squishy slop.

Heron had spotted him too.
Hungrily she tippy-toed closer, stopping and cocking her head directly above the little froglet.

Help! I'm stuck!

He's not going to make it!

Chapter 8

Suddenly two things happened at once:
A razor-sharp beak flashed like
a spear and Splodge was gone!

And, at that very moment, the
terrified tadpoles and froglets heard
a deafening screeching noise.

Heron heard it too and
froze in her tracks.

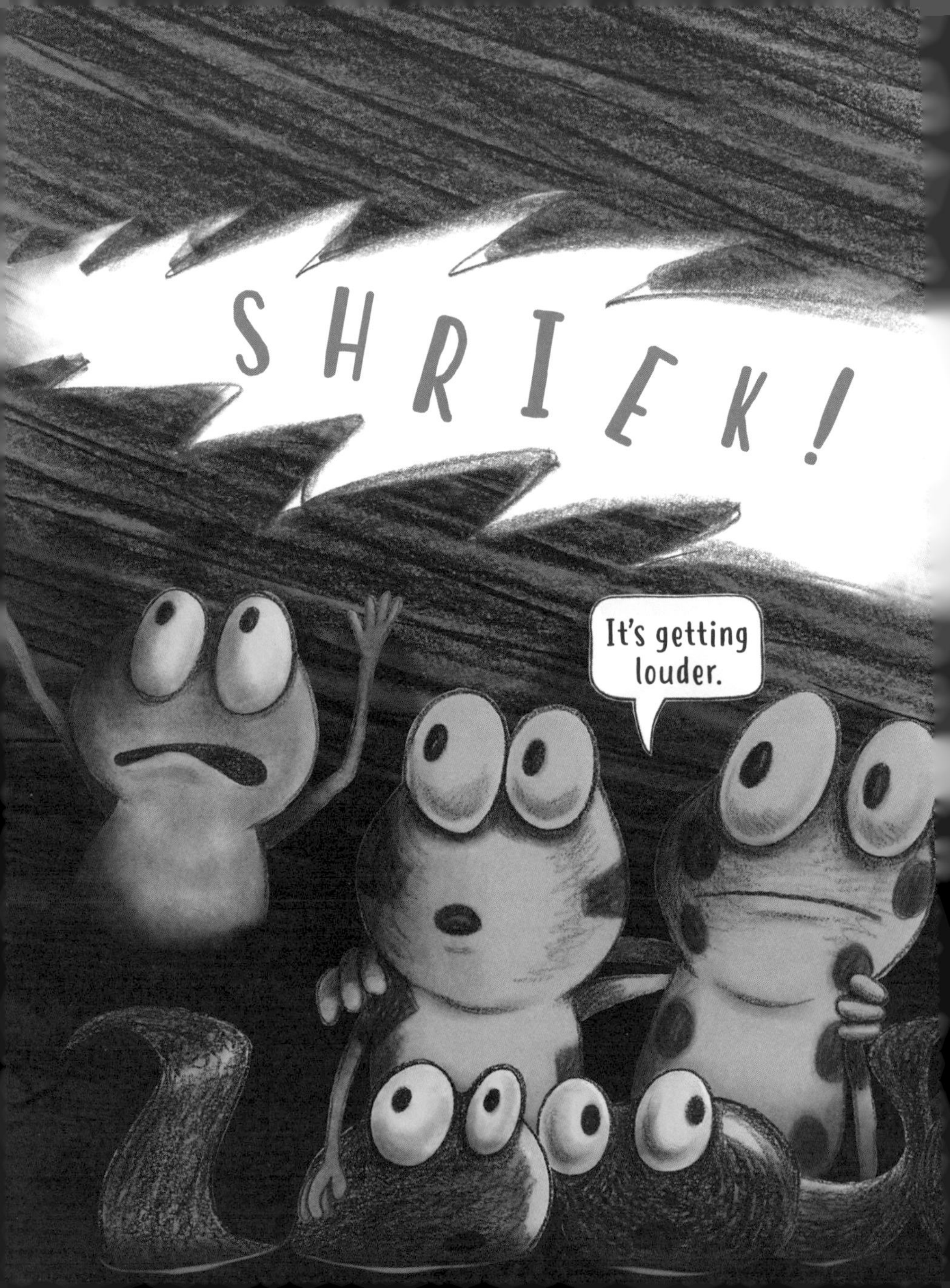
SHRIEK!
It's getting louder.

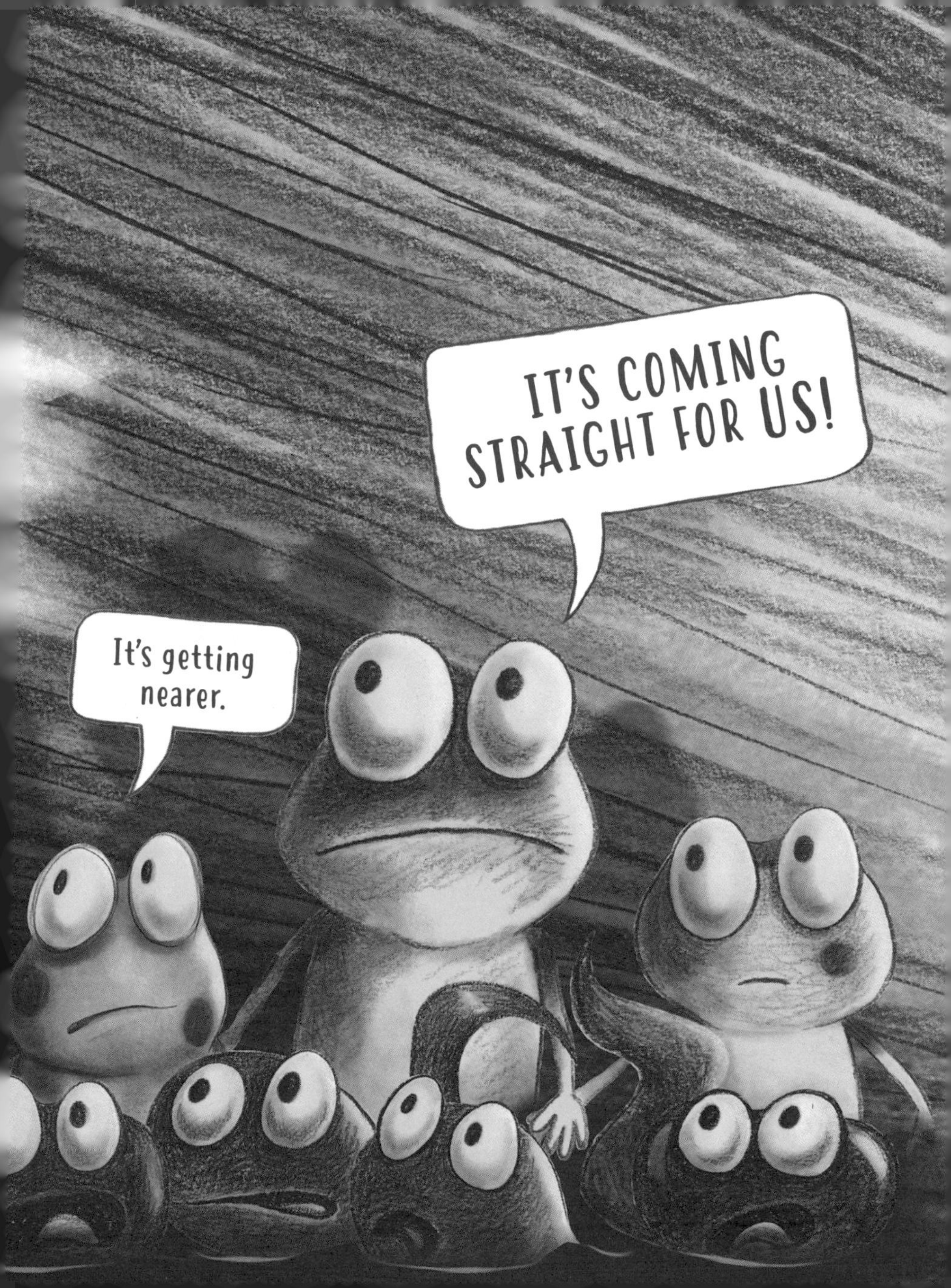
It's getting nearer.
IT'S COMING STRAIGHT FOR US!

Out of the dead, dark depths of the log

rushed . . .

Well, it was definitely the strangest, craziest goggle-eyed creature they had ever seen. It hurtled over them and raced straight at Heron.

Yaaaaaarlp!

Heron stumbled back. Then in a flapping frenzy she flew off, spitting and spluttering, and dropping Splodge

Bug Belly threw off his Heron-scarer disguise and rushed to help up the stunned little froglet.

"Hey, are you OK?" he asked Splodge.

Splodge nodded, still in a daze.

"My plan worked even better than I'd imagined," said Bug Belly, "but **WOW** that was **CLOSE!** Splish, did you finish—"

Bug Belly stopped mid-sentence. The taddies who had squirmed out of the log, were now flailing about, stuck in the gloop. **"HELP!"** they cried.

My bum's stuck!

Chapter 9

"Aw buttered beetles! The pond's nearly empty!" exclaimed Bug Belly.

He thought quickly.

"Splish, Splash, Splodge, help the taddies over to this last little puddle. Hurry!" he ordered. "Or they'll be stuck forever like mini mud statues!"

"We're not going to get out!" wailed the taddies.

"Trust me," said Bug Belly, "this is the cleverest bit of my plan."

BUG BELLY'S CLEVEREST PLAN part 3

TUBE SLIDE ESCAPE

Slot all stalks together
to make one LONG tube slide.

219 taddies √
23 froglets √
1 PIKE!
1 HERON
* SNAKE?

Taddies' section

Bug Belly's section

Last puddle
of water

Top Pond
(Emptying!)

Middle Pond
(Old Snapper!)

Bottom Pond
(Safety!)

* When should I tell them about the snake?

Bug Belly disappeared over the edge of Top Pond and quickly connected the taddies' hollow stalk tube to his own, making one long tube, leading all the way down to Bottom Pond.

"Ta-da!" he exclaimed. "**This is your chute to safety.**"

He was interrupted by a loud **SQUELCH** and a huge **SLURP!**

The water in the tiny puddle was almost gone . . .

The tadpoles were getting sucked into the MUD!

"Eeeek!" the taddies panicked.

They jostled and jiggled in a frenzied crush to be first down the slide.

"Hey, stop pushing!" cried one.

"Me first!" said a small taddie.

"No, me!" said another.

Bug Belly needed to act fast.

"Whoa, wait! Hold on, everyone!"
Bug Belly shouted. **"STOP!"**

"Before **ANYONE** shoots down the slide, we first need to send down some of this."

With a wicked grin, Bug Belly scraped together a huge, sloppy pile of smelly **duck poo**.

He squelched it into the slide and sent it sloshing down to Bottom Pond.

"Eeeeeeeugh, what on earth is that for?" the taddies squealed in disgust.

"I'll explain later," winked Bug Belly. "QUICKLY now. There's just enough water left to wash YOU down the slide. Keep swimming, keep going until you reach Bottom Pond. And be EXTRA careful when you come out of the other end! Taddies first."

Chapter 10

Bug Belly told Splish and the other froglets to wait until every last tadpole had whooshed down the tubes.

"And then get yourselves down to Bottom Pond too."

And with that, he hopped off.

"Where's he going now?!" cried Splash.

"Forget it," cried Splish. "There's no time to lose! GO, GO, GO!"

The taddies quickly grasped the idea and
launched themselves into the tube-rider slide.
It was brilliant fun.

One by one, each little black blob slid down and out of the slide **PLIP!** into Bottom Pond, **PLOP!**

They squealed with laughter.

When all the taddies and froglets had arrived safely, Bug Belly, who was too big to fit in the slide, was waiting.

"Welcome to your new home!" he exclaimed.

"ANYONE... READY... FOR... MORE ... FROGGY FUN?!"

"We are!" everyone yelled.

With a few spare tubes and some Bug Belly ingenuity they built a super

mini water slide extravaganza!

Everyone had great fun splashing around until their mums and dads came to collect them.

The taddies all clamoured round Bug Belly shouting:

"This was the best day EVER!"

"Can Uncle Bug Belly babysit us EVERY DAY?"

"Pleeease? Pleeeeeease?"

But then Splash couldn't help blabbing about them nearly being gobbled up in a three-course pike dinner . . . And how Splodge was speared by Heron . . . And how they all got stuck like mud statues.

Bug Belly hastily explained about how

they'd ended up in Bottom Pond. Luckily, the parents were so amazed at his brilliant plan, they forgot to be angry.

That was until Splodge piped up, "What about the duck poo, Uncle Bug Belly?"

Chapter 11

"Duck poo?" the mums and dads exclaimed, horrified.

"Duck poo?"

"Ah, yes, the duck poo." Bug Belly grinned. "Well you see, Sneaky Snake had been snooping around Bottom Pond and watching our every move. I had an awful feeling that she might be waiting at the end of the slide to snatch a tasty taddie snack.

"Well, if she was, she will have had the surprise of her life and a very nasty, smelly surprise too!"

Yeeeeuuurgh!

Everyone thought that was the funniest thing ever.

And Bug Belly would have joined in too, except he was suddenly distracted when a **snack** buzzed by and his tummy went . . .

LOOK OUT FOR MORE FUN

BUG BELLY

ADVENTURES
COMING SOON!

Find me in Bug Belly's kit bag on p. 44.